Michelle Robinson

ODD SOCKS

Rebecca Ashdown

A pair of new socks came to live in a drawer.
"It's perfect," said Suki. "We couldn't want more."
"Exactly," said Sosh to his warm, woolly wife.
"A match made in heaven! Now, this is the life."

The two went to work on
a fresh pair of feet.
They fitted just perfectly.
"Isn't this neat?"

They ran to the
roundabout,

whizzed down the slide.

They stopped for an ice cream
and went for a ride.

In jellies,

in wellies,

and into the wash.

"I love hanging out with you, Suki," said Sosh.

Tucked in the drawer at the end of each day,
they'd curl up together and Suki would say:

"Just you and me, darling, we never will part.
Your threads are entwined in my warm, woolly heart."

But then, late one night
in their laundry room bed,
Sosh spotted something that
filled him with dread.

Something quite tiny on Suki's big toe.

"A little hole, Suki!"

"Oh, darn it!"

UH OH...

The hole became BIGGER. The wind whistled through it.
A voice said, "You're done for, that's all there is to it."
Big Bob was an old sock, a real winter woolly –
a loner, a moaner, a bit of a bully.

"I've seen it before with my first woolly wife –
that hole was the start of the end of her life.
It started out small but she soon fell apart.
You're bound for the bin."

"Gosh," said Sosh, "have a heart!
Don't listen, my darling – calm down, now. There, there.
Chuck such a super sock? They wouldn't dare."

But later that day
in the back of
the drawer...

"Where's Suki?" Sosh said.
"She was right here before."
"You've lost her," Big Bob said,
"I wish it weren't true, but I see an
ODD SOCK when I look at you.
Find someone else, Sosh.
Don't go it alone."

But Sosh wouldn't have it.
"I'm one of a pair!
My wife's out there somewhere.
I'll find her, I swear!"

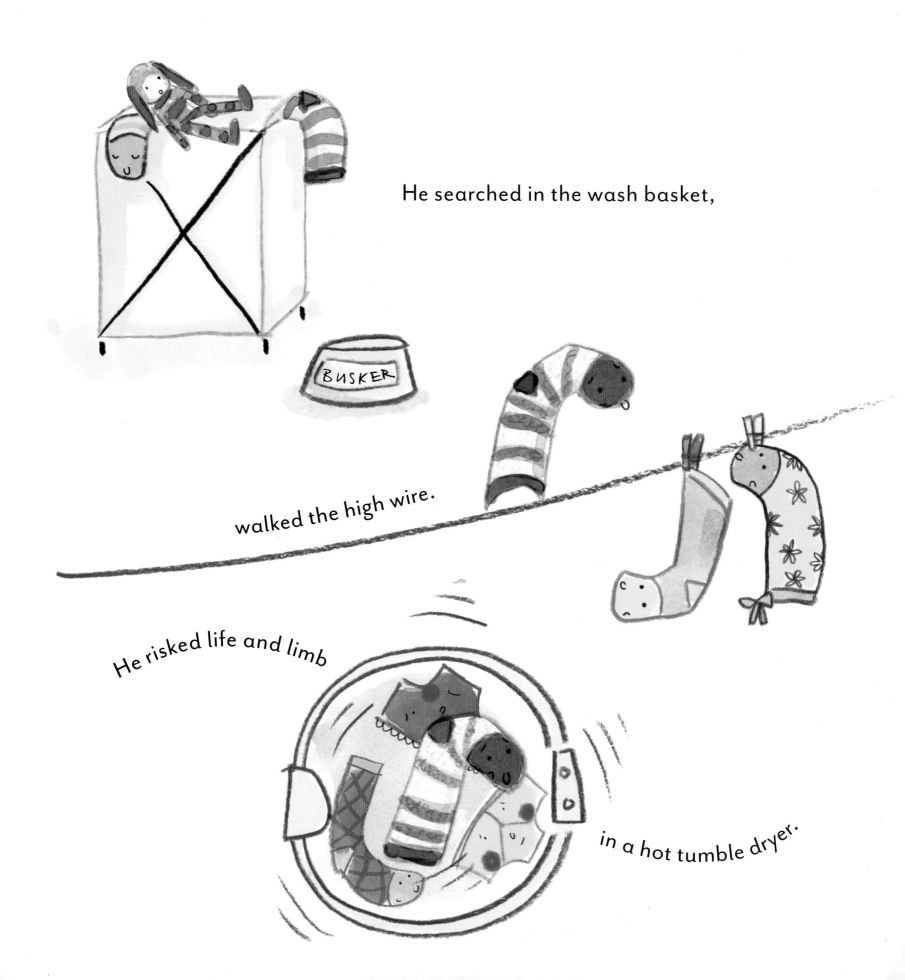

He searched in the wash basket,

BUSKER

walked the high wire.

He risked life and limb

in a hot tumble dryer.

He tried on the trampoline,
bounced back inside.

Checked under the sofa...

"Just dust, Love – I've tried."

He'd found an old slipper
who'd lost her own mate.

"Please find him," she pleaded, "before it's too late."

Sosh froze on the spot as the dog wandered through –
it had something holey... and fluffy... and blue!

WALKIES!

The dog ran off.

"Suki?!" Sosh cried.

He peered in the basket.
She wasn't inside.
But *someone* was...

Sosh said,
"You're coming with me."

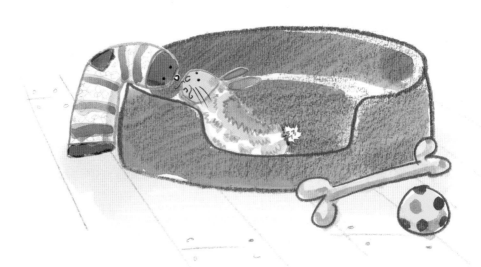

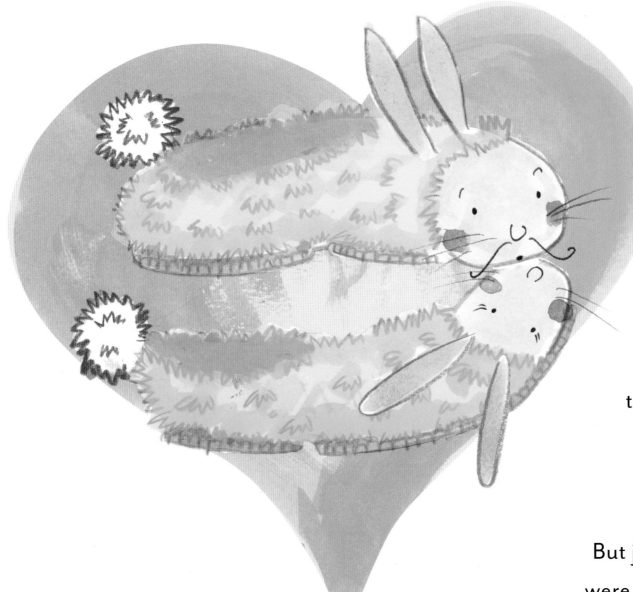

"Our hero!"
the slipper said.
"Sweetheart,
I'm free!"

But just as the slippers
were having a smooch...

Sosh was whisked off by that pedigree pooch!

He watched his whole life flash by – WHOOSH – just like that.

"Why couldn't the family have chosen a cat?! I'm practically new – why, I've barely been worn! Now there's just one of me..."

Sosh came around.

He was broken and sore.

Where was he? The waste bin? It wasn't the drawer.

"I've lost her," he cried. "When the going got tough,

I gave it my best, but it wasn't enough."

"Suki!" he moaned in the darkness. "My love!"

"Open your eyes,"
came a voice from above...

"You found me, my darling!"
his dear Suki said,
new googly eyes popping
out of her head.

"Do you remember: the glitter? The glue?
We'll never part now, my love, not me and you."

"A match made in heaven – now this is the life!"
said sock puppet Sosh to his sock puppet wife.

And that's where we'll leave them, at home in their box.
A perfectly fine pair of VERY odd socks!